R...

Written by Jack Gabolinscy

Look at these animals.
They are all rats.
Look at all the colors
a rat can be.

Rats can live in a lot of places. Some rats live in the wild and some rats live by the water. Some rats live in houses, too.

Rats can grow very big.
They have a long tail and
big, big teeth.
Their teeth are very,
very sharp!

teeth

0 inches   20 inches

Rats can be very big.

Rats will eat all the food
that they can get.
They will eat garbage, too.

fruit and
vegetables

wires

bread

soap

A mother rat can have lots and lots of babies. She can have hundreds of baby rats in a year.

When the baby rats are born,
they have no hair.
Their eyes are shut,
and they cannot see.

Some people don't like rats.
Rats can be pests.
They make holes in things
with their teeth.
They take food from houses.
They carry germs, too.

But not all rats are pests!
This is a pet rat.
It lives in a cage and plays
on a wheel.

Index

Guide Notes

> **Title: Rats**
> **Stage:** Early (3) – Blue
>
> **Genre:** Nonfiction
> **Approach:** Guided Reading
> **Processes:** Thinking Critically, Exploring Language, Processing Information
> **Written and Visual Focus:** Photographs (static images), Index, Label, Caption, Scale Diagram

THINKING CRITICALLY
(sample questions)

- Look at the front cover and the title. Ask the children what they know about rats.
- Look at the title and read it to the children.
- Focus the children's attention on the index. Ask: "What are you going to find out about in this book?"
- Ask the children what they know about the food a rat likes to eat.
- If you want to find out about the food a rat eats, what page would you look on?
- If you want to find out about a rat's babies, what page would you look on?
- Look at pages 4 and 5. Why do you think rats are able to live in lots of different places?
- Look at pages 12 and 13. Why do you think rats could carry germs?

EXPLORING LANGUAGE

Terminology
Title, cover, photographs, author, photographers

Vocabulary
Interest words: sharp, teeth, grow, garbage, pests, germs, places
High-frequency words: very, don't, these, take, that
Positional words: in, on, by
Compound word: cannot

Print Conventions
Capital letter for sentence beginnings, periods, commas, exclamation marks